To my older brother, Paul, for showing me stuff. D.B.
For my old mate Peter, thanks for all your help and support. S.L.

OXFORD
UNIVERSITY PRESS

Great Clarendon Street, Oxford OX2 6DP

Oxford University Press is a department of the University of Oxford.
It furthers the University's objective of excellence in research, scholarship,
and education by publishing worldwide in

Oxford New York

Auckland Cape Town Dar es Salaam Hong Kong Karachi
Kuala Lumpur Madrid Melbourne Mexico City Nairobi
New Delhi Shanghai Taipei Toronto

With offices in

Argentina Austria Brazil Chile Czech Republic France Greece
Guatemala Hungary Italy Japan Poland Portugal Singapore
South Korea Switzerland Thailand Turkey Ukraine Vietnam

Oxford is a registered trade mark of Oxford University Press
in the UK and in certain other countries

Text © David Bedford 2005
Illustrations © Steve Lavis 2005

The moral rights of the author and artist have been asserted

Database right Oxford University Press (maker)

First published 2005

British Library Cataloguing in Publication Data available

ISBN–13: 978–019-279148-1 (Hardback)
ISBN–10: 0-19-279148-6 (Hardback)
ISBN–13: 978–019-272533-2 (Paperback)
ISBN–10: 0-19-272533-5 (Paperback)

1 3 5 7 9 10 8 6 4 2

Printed in China

Max
and Sadie

DAVID BEDFORD AND STEVE LAVIS

OXFORD
UNIVERSITY PRESS

It was a bright new morning.
Max yawned and stretched.
'Mum, can we go for a swim?'
'Sorry,' said Mum. 'I can't swim now.
I have to give little Sadie her breakfast.'

Max didn't mind.
He liked floating quietly by himself.

But suddenly . . .

Splash!

Sadie squealed. 'Can I swim with you, Max?'
'No,' said Max.
'Why not?' said Sadie.
'Because I'm happy on my own,'
said Max, and he swam away.

Later, Max dug a hole for a new snow den.
'Mum, will you help me pat the walls flat?'
'Sorry,' said Mum. 'I need to wash Sadie's paws.
Can you make a den by yourself now?'

Max patted
the walls on his own.
He'd only just finished when . . .

Crash!

Sadie jumped through the roof.
She giggled. 'Will you show
me how to make a den, Max?'
'No!' said Max.
'Why not?' asked Sadie.
'Because you spoil everything!'
said Max, and he stomped away.

Max walked and walked. He didn't know where
he was going. He just wanted to get away from Sadie.

Over a hill, he found a field
of crisp, new snow. 'Good!' said Max.
He liked being the first to make footprints.

But before he took a step . . .

Crunch!

Sadie skipped, and
danced, and kicked
through the new snow.
'I followed you!' she said.
'Show me how fast you can
run on the snow, Max.'

'All right,' said Max. 'I will!' And he ran across the
snow field as fast as he could, so that Sadie
would never catch him up.

Max ran and ran, until Sadie was out of sight.
Then he looked up, and saw dark clouds
racing across the sky. 'Oh no!'
said Max. 'A snow storm!'

Max quickly built
a snow den and
curled up inside,
safe and warm.

Then he remembered Sadie.
Was she still on the snow field,
all alone?

He crawled out into
the falling snow
to look for her.

Bump!

A heavy lump knocked Max over.

'I followed your footprints!' said Sadie, laughing.

'Get off!' said Max. 'We can't play now.'

'Why not?' said Sadie.

'Because there's a snow storm coming!' said Max.

'I need to make a bigger den to fit you inside.'

'Let me help,' said Sadie.

'I promise I won't spoil it.'

Sadie was good
at scooping out the
snow the way Max showed her.
The den was soon big enough for
them both to squeeze inside – just in time.

Max held Sadie close as the storm howled outside.
'I want Mummy,' said Sadie.

'Don't worry,' said Max.
'She'll find us.'

Sadie was snoring when Mum came.
'Shall I wake her?' whispered Max.
'Let her sleep,' said Mum. 'We can stay up late
together, and watch the stars come out.
Just like we used to.'

'Look!' said Max. 'The sky colours are flashing.
I want to show Sadie.'

Gently, Max woke his little sister.

'What do the colours mean?' said Sadie.
'They mean we're going to have a good
day tomorrow,' said Max.
'Can I go swimming with you?'
'Yes,' said Max.
'And build a den?' said Sadie.
'If you don't jump through the roof!'
said Max, laughing.
'Wow!' said Sadie. 'You're
brilliant, Max!'

'Yes,' said Mum . . .

'Max *is* brilliant.'
And she cuddled Max and Sadie
together as they drifted
off to sleep.